Sultana's Sandals

Illustrated by
Claudine Gévry

ROWLAND READING FOUNDATION
MADISON, WISCONSIN

ar	er	others	ir	oy
far	after	perfect	dirty	annoy
hard	another	perhaps	girl	annoyed
harder	better	potter	twirled	annoying
market	bother	river	whirling	boy
start	clattered	scattered	**ur**	enjoy
started	desert	seller	hurt	
or	everyone	sister	returned	Trickers
for	gather	slippers	returning	**ear, or**
forever	harder	together	surprised	heard
morning	her	under	**oi**	Pearl
Morocco	herself	whatever	disappointed	work
or	merchants	wondered	pointed	worked
story	never			world

he'll   I'll   she'll   they'll   we'll   you'll

know   does   laugh   both   again
kind   buy   find   right   wash   light

blow   foolish   friends   old   Once

This tale is from Morocco. Morocco is in Africa.
The days are long and hot. After the sun sets,
friends gather together. They tell tales from
long ago, like this tale.

Once there was a girl who was a potter. Her name was Sultana. Sultana had a pair of sandals that she liked very, very much.

The left sandal was held together with a bit of string. The right sandal was patched and mended so much, all that was left were patches and mends.

But the sandals fit Sultana like soft slippers.
They never rubbed or hurt or pinched or
flopped. Sultana liked her sandals,
and did not want to buy any others.

"I think these are the only sandals for me,"
she said to herself.

But her friends did not think so. They pointed
at her sandals and laughed.

"How can you stand those awful, dirty sandals?"
asked Fatima, the melon seller.

"Those sandals look awfully foolish on you,"
said Hassan, the fig seller.

"Why don't you get rid of those patched-
together sandals?" asked Kassim, a boy
who worked on a fishing boat.

"Those sandals make you look like a camel and
run like a mule," giggled Sultana's sister, Yasmin.

Sultana heard what they said. But she just smiled.
She liked her sandals. "I think they are the best
sandals in the world," she said.
"They are perfect for me."

So Sultana's friends got together and surprised her with a gift. It was a new pair of sandals. The new sandals were light and clean and polished.

"These are fine sandals," Sultana said to her friends. "I'll enjoy them. I thank you."

"We'll enjoy seeing your feet in them!" said her friends.

But to herself Sultana said, "These new sandals are far too stiff and hard. They'll pinch my toes. They'll hurt my feet. I'll miss my old, patched-together sandals."

Sultana looked at the new, perfectly polished sandals.

"I can tell that Sultana is very thankful for her fine sandals," said Fatima, the melon seller. "She'll like them so much better than the old ones."

"Yes! She thinks they are so fine that all she can do is stare at them," said Kassim, the fishing boy.

All of Sultana's friends felt very good
about their gift. They smiled at Sultana.

"You'll look so much better in the new sandals
we gave you," they said.

After her friends left, Sultana began to think. "I still prefer my old, patched-together sandals," she said to herself. "But my friends were kind to buy these new ones for me. They'll be disappointed if I don't get rid of the old sandals."

So Sultana sadly put her old sandals in the river.

"I hope another girl will find them and use them and like them as much as I do," she said.

The sandals bobbed and drifted and floated away. They looked like small, sad ships.

The next day, when Kassim the fishing boy gathered in his net, he was surprised. There were both of Sultana's old sandals mixed in with the fish!

"I don't want those sandals tangled up in my net!" he said.

Kassim untangled the sandals. He returned them to Sultana.

"Don't put these in the river again," he said. "I don't want them annoying the fish."

"So, my dear sandals are back," said Sultana to herself. "I still think they are the only sandals for me! And now they are washed clean from being in the river. But I know that my friends will be disappointed if I don't get rid of them. What can I do with them?"

While she was thinking, Sultana put the wet sandals in the sun to dry. Yasmin's cat, Pearl, started to play with them.

Pearl the cat tossed the sandals playfully.
They landed right in front of Fatima,
the melon seller. Flop! Fatima tripped
on the sandals! Plonk! Fatima dropped her
basket of melons. The melons fell into the dust.

When Sultana saw the fuss, she rushed outside to help Fatima pick up the melons.

Fatima plunked the sandals in Sultana's hands. "Foolish girl!" she said. "Why don't you get rid of these patched-together sandals?"

"I tried," said Sultana. "Ask Kassim. He'll tell you that I put the sandals in the river. But somehow they came back to me."

"Try harder," said Fatima.

Sultana said to her, "I will."

But to herself Sultana said, "So, my dear sandals are back. I still think they are the only sandals for me. And now they are washed clean from being in the river and dry from being in the sun. But if I don't get rid of them, all my friends will be mad at me. What can I do with them?"

Sultana had to come up with another plan. How was she to get rid of the sandals? She wondered and wondered. All of a sudden, she smiled. She jumped out of bed, picked up the patched-together sandals, and ran to the big gate by the market.

Sultana scrambled to the top of the gate. She stuffed her sandals in a crack.

"This is a good spot for my patched-together sandals," she said to herself. "They can stay here forever. Nothing will bother them here."

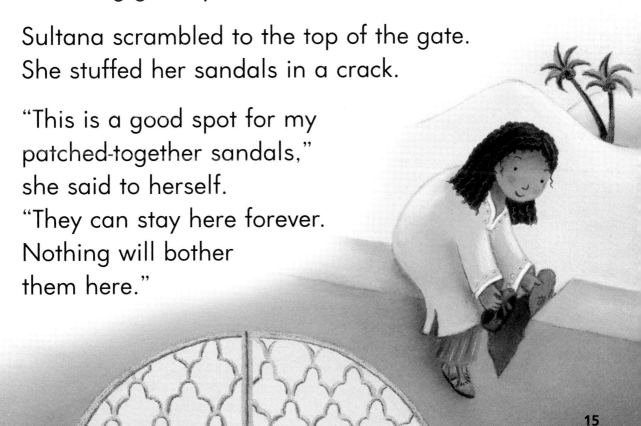

The next morning, the merchants began to set up stands under the gate.

There was Fatima with her baskets of melons, Kassim with his fish, and Hassan with his figs. There was a stand selling chickens, another selling baskets, another selling rugs, and another selling cakes.

There was a wagon filled with sticks next to mules for sale.

A brisk wind began to blow. It whipped up
and in and under and past the sandals.
All of a sudden, the wind lifted
Sultana's old sandals out of the
crack. It swept them up and
sent them whirling and flying.
They skipped and twisted
and twirled in the wind.

Then plop! They landed on the littlest mule's back.

"Heeeehaaaaw! Heeeehaaaw!" the littlest mule squawked. He kicked and bucked and jumped. In a second, all the other mules began to kick and buck, too. They broke the rope that held them. They crashed into the wagon and all the sticks scattered. The mules stomped on the sticks and kicked up the dust.

Stands toppled over. Chickens flapped and fussed. Fish went flying. Rugs landed on baskets. Pots and pans clattered. The mules ran off into the desert, braying and squealing.

Fatima was annoyed. Hassan was confused.
Kassim was amazed. Oh, what a mess
it was! No one had ever seen such a
terrible mess before!

When the dust settled, everyone began
to put the stands back together again.
As he cleaned up the mess, Hassan
held up the patched-together sandals.

"Look!" cried Hassan. "Are these Sultana's sandals?
Can these be the rascals that made this mess?
I think they are!"

"Those are Sultana's old sandals!" said Kassim.
"They got tangled up in my fishing net!"

"Those are the sandals that tripped me
and made me spill my melons!" said Fatima.

"But how did they get here?" asked Yasmin.

"And how can we get rid of them?"
asked Hassan.

"Whatever you do, don't put them in the river where they will annoy the fish!" said Kassim.

"And don't put them in the sun so that my cat Pearl will play with them," said Yasmin.

"And don't put them where they will trip me and make me spill my melons," said Fatima.

"And don't put them where they will fly out and land on a mule and start a big fuss in the market," said Hassan.

They all began to think.

Then Yasmin said, "Perhaps the best thing to do is to ask Sultana to put them back on her feet."

"Yes!" said Fatima. "We are safe from them when Sultana has them on."

"That is a good plan," said Kassim.

So Sultana's friends washed off the old sandals. They gave them back to Sultana.

"We are returning these sandals to you," said Hassan. "May we ask you to put them on your feet again? Life just does not work unless they are on your feet."

Sultana put her old, patched-together sandals back on her feet where they belonged. She put her other sandals in a box in her closet.

"Ahh!" Sultana said. "These old sandals feel so good! They do not pinch or hurt or flop. They are perfect for me."

All of Sultana's friends were very glad.

"As long as Sultana is standing on those sandals, they will not bother us," said Yasmin.

Everyone smiled happily.

Sultana's smile was the happiest of all. "These are the only sandals for me!" she said.

Everyone agreed.

And that is the end of this story from long ago and far away!